Meeting Pickles

Story by Carmel Reilly

Illustrations by Pat Reynolds

Contents

Chapter 1

The New Puppy

Eddie patted Pickles.

"Pickles is so funny," said Nina.
"He likes to play all the time."

Eddie was Nina's best friend.
He lived next door,
and he had come
to see her new puppy.

Pickles jumped up at Eddie
and barked.

"Sit, Pickles," said Eddie. "Sit!"

But Pickles kept jumping up
and barking at him.

Nina laughed.
"He likes you, Eddie," she said.
"Come here, Pickles."

Pickles looked at Nina and barked.
Then he ran away.

Nina tried to catch him,
but every time she got close,
he would run away again.

Eddie began to chase Pickles, too.

Chapter 2

Too Fast

"Get him, Eddie," cried Nina.
"Get him before he goes inside the house.
Mum does not like him running
in the house."

Away they went after Pickles,
but he was too fast for them.

Pickles raced up the steps
and in the back door.

"Oh, no!" Nina said to Eddie.
"We can't chase him inside the house.
Mum will be very cross with us!"

"She will be very cross with Pickles, too,"
said Eddie.

Just then,
Pickles came racing out of the house
with something in his mouth.

"Stop him, Eddie!" shouted Nina.
"What has he got in his mouth?"

"It's a shoe!" shouted Eddie.

"It's one of my **new** school shoes,"
cried Nina.
"I left my shoes on the floor
by my school bag!"

Chapter 3

Put that Shoe Down

Pickles sat down
and began to chew Nina's shoe.

Nina walked slowly up to him.
"Pickles!" she said.
"Put my shoe down.
Good dog, Pickles."

Mum came out of the house
and saw Pickles with Nina's new shoe.
Mum was not very pleased at all.

"Pickles needs to go to puppy school,"
said Eddie.
Pickles looked at Eddie and barked.
Nina's shoe fell onto the grass.

"Yes," said Nina, laughing.
She picked up her shoe.
"We will have to take him to puppy school
as soon as we can!"